P9-DFQ-535

Contents

igloobooks

Published in 2016
by Igloo Books Ltd
Cottage Farm
Sywell
Northants
NN6 0BJ
www.igloobooks.com

LEO002 0516
2 4 6 8 10 9 7 5 3 1
ISBN: 978-1-78670-029-2

Printed and manufactured in China
Illustrated by Jack Hughes
Stories by Joff Brown

5 Minute Tales
Stories for Boys

igloobooks

Danny and the Dozy Dinosaur

Danny was the luckiest boy in the world. He had a pet dinosaur. His name was Rex, and he was very big and very friendly. Rex followed Danny everywhere, even to school. Rex even slept in Danny's bedroom at night.

However, there was only one problem with having a pet dinosaur. Rex snored and it was very, very loud.

Have you ever heard a dinosaur snore? It's louder than a zooming car, louder than an express train, louder than a jumbo jet taking off!

Rex snored so loudly, it made Danny's bed shake. It rattled all the shingles on the roofs of the houses in the street. It kept all the neighbors awake at night.

"We've got to do something about your snoring!" Danny said to Rex. The question was, what?

"I know," said Danny. "Maybe if you eat a lot, your tummy will be so full, you won't be able to snore!"

So, that night, Danny gave Rex burgers, hot dogs, and a stack of pork chops. Rex gobbled them up and went straight to sleep.

At first there was silence, but then Rex went, "BURP!" It was even louder than his snoring. "BUUUURP!" Rex did it again. It was so loud, the room shook.

The next night, Danny borrowed his brother's electric guitar. "Some music might make you sleep quietly," he told Rex. Danny began to play.

A terrible sound came from the guitar, it was like a screeching cat. The noise echoed down the street. When Danny started to sing, it was even worse. Rex put his paws over his ears it was so bad. He couldn't wait to go to sleep. Then, when he finally did, Rex snored louder than ever!

Danny took Rex to the doctor. Rex could hardly fit into the doctor's office. The doctor took Rex's temperature (he broke the thermometer by accident) and felt Rex's pulse.

"I think that Rex snores because he's uncomfortable in your small bedroom," said the doctor. "If he lies outside with his head on a pillow, perhaps he will stop snoring."

So, Danny's mom made Rex a huge, foam pillow. It was as big as Danny's bed! That night, when Rex came into Danny's room to sleep, Danny told him he had to go outside.

Rex rested his head on the huge pillow, but he didn't like sleeping outside, it was lonely and cold.

Danny woke the next morning to the sound of gigantic hiccups. He looked out of the window and saw Rex standing near ripped pieces of foam. Rex had chewed up his pillow in his sleep! He looked very sorry for himself.

Danny noticed all the little pieces of foam on the ground. Suddenly, he had an idea. "I think I have a brilliant use for those pieces of foam," he said.

That night, Rex slept back in Danny's warm bedroom. He snored louder than ever, but this time no one minded. Danny had made earplugs from all the pillow foam Rex had chewed. He could snore as loudly as he liked and no one could hear him! At last, everyone got a good night's sleep.

Captain Percy

Captain Black Bear was the captain of the pirate ship, The Black Claw. He was fierce and mean. He hoarded the treasure that the pirates stole and made them work very hard on the ship. They had to scrub the deck, make his food, and hoist the heavy mainsail. Captain Black Bear, however, never did any work himself.

The captain's parrot, Percy, was just as unhappy as the crew. All day long, he sat on his master's shoulder. If he so much as squawked, he was told to be quiet. "Captain Black Bear never lets me do anything," he muttered quietly to himself. "If only we could have another captain. We need someone clever and adventurous— someone like ME!"

Percy thought and thought until he came up with a plan. He waited until Black Bear wasn't looking, then stole the key to the treasure room. Later on, when the captain was inspecting his treasure, Percy grabbed Black Bear's hat and his long cutlass. He squawked as loudly as he could and flapped out of the door.

"What are you doing, you feathered fool!" roared Black Bear. Percy just squawked and slammed the door, then locked it behind him. The fearsome captain was trapped!

Percy quickly flew up on deck and called to the crew. "At last we are free of Captain Black Bear!" he squawked.

"Captain Black Bear is a traitor!" squawked Percy, so all the pirates could hear. "He sailed away in the night, mateys. Now *I'm* the captain of this ship."

The crew were very happy. "The villain has gone!" they cried. Captain Percy and the crew celebrated with a very merry party. They ate all the food and drank all the coconut water.

No one did any work for two whole days. Life without Captain Black Bear was lots of fun. Nobody did any repairs to the ship. They ate and drank as much as they wanted. They didn't even bother to steer the ship. It was great fun doing what they liked. Everyone just had a great, lazy time!

Soon, however, the food ran out and the crew were lost in the middle of the ocean. To make things worse, the ship was in such bad shape that water was beginning to leak into it. "It's all that parrot's fault," the crew cried. "It's time we got rid of Captain Percy!"

They tied up Percy and made him walk the plank. "Wait!" cried Percy.
"Captain Black Bear didn't really sail away. He's locked in the treasure room."

The pirates rushed down to the treasure room and broke the door in. There was
Captain Black Bear, looking very sorry for himself. All he'd had to eat for days
were dry, crumbly cookies.

The crew were so glad to see their old captain, they all cheered. But, when Captain Black Bear saw the mess on deck, he was very angry. "Back to work, boys!" he cried. "There's lots to do!"

Instead of complaining, the pirates rushed back to work. They repaired the leaky hull, steered the ship safely, and stopped eating and drinking so much.

Even Captain Black Bear was happy when he saw how hard they were working. The pirates were happy, too.

As for Percy, Captain Black Bear made him scrub the decks until they shone. Percy didn't mind though. "I'd rather scrub planks than walk off them!" he laughed. At last, everyone on board The Black Claw was happy.

Fright Night

Jamie pushed open the door of the spooky old house on the hill.
"I dare you to go in," said his friend, Connor. "I bet it's haunted."
"No one lives here," said Jamie, "and I don't believe in ghosts."
He stepped into the dark hallway.

Suddenly, a shadow moved behind them. There was a weird clanking noise.
"Look out!" cried Connor.

CRASSSH! A suit of armor nearly fell on top of them. The noise echoed all around. "Wow, that was close," said Connor. "It's a good job we got out of the way. It must have been knocked when the door opened."

Jamie felt a thrill of excitement. There was something strange about this house and he wanted to find out what. "Come on," he said. "Let's go and explore."

23

Inside, the house was damp and dark. Suddenly, a gust of cold wind made the hairs on Connor's neck stand up. "I don't like this," he said. "Maybe the house really is haunted. Perhaps we should go."

Suddenly, out of nowhere, something flapped against his face. It touched his shoulder.

"Something's got me!" screamed Connor, waving his arms, frantically.
Jamie burst out laughing. "It's just a silly curtain," he said.

Connor turned to see a curtain flapping in the wind that blew through a broken
window. He tried not to look scared. "Come on," said Jamie. "Let's see what
other spooky things we can find."

On the first floor they found a strange room. The walls were lined with old paintings, whose eyes seemed to follow them around.

Jamie noticed a pair of green eyes looking out from a dark alcove. "I saw them move," he said, shivering. "I'm scared!"
"Stop being so jumpy," said Connor. But, when he looked closer, he saw the eyes blink.

The strange eyes blinked again. Then, they started to move.
"Oh, no! They're coming closer," said Jamie.
Then, a black shape leapt out. "Look out!" shouted Connor.

"Ahhhh!" cried Connor and Jamie, running up the staircase. The black shape followed them. But it was only a black cat with big, green eyes!
"Meow!" went the cat, purring gently. It wasn't scary at all.

"Ha-ha! You should have seen your face," said Connor. "You looked terrified."
"So did you," said Jamie. "You ran up the stairs faster than I did!"

Keeping very close together, the two friends crept into the next room.

The room was full of clothes that glowed with a strange light. Suddenly, a big gust of wind blew through the room. The clothes began to move. The arms on the shirts began to stretch out, then the shirts flew off the hangers.

Connor and Jamie looked at one another. Had they finally found ghosts? They weren't about to hang around and find out.

"RUUUUNNN!" shouted Jamie. He and Connor dashed down the staircase. They tore along the corridor, across the hall, and out through the open front door.

"I'm sure it was just the wind," said Jamie. Connor nodded his head. "There's no such thing as ghosts." They both turned and looked at the top of the house. "Or is there?"

29

Space Race

The most exciting place in the world for Jack and Josh was the Space Lab.
Their dad worked there and today they were allowed to visit.
Whoosh! Vroom! went a rocket from the launch pad.

"Wow!" cried Josh, as he walked behind his dad. "That's amazing!"
"Wouldn't it be cool if we could be real astronauts?" said Jack,
as he followed his little brother and their dad inside.

Dad was busy and he disappeared into a laboratory. Jack looked around and pointed at a door that said: 'ROCKET TESTING. DO NOT ENTER.'
He gave a big grin and opened the door.

Inside was an incredible rocket. Jack climbed into it. "I wonder what this does?" he asked, pressing a big, green button.
"No, don't!" cried Josh, but it was too late. There was a deep rumble. The rocket engines had started.

With a thunderous roar, the rocket shot into the sky. It zoomed, super fast, up through the clouds and into space. Josh and Jack were amazed. They whizzed past meteorites. They sped past space crafts, faster and faster. But what if they couldn't get back to Earth?

Jack saw a big, red button. "Please don't press it," cried Josh. "What if it blows the ship up, or ejects us into space?"

"There's only one way to find out!" said Jack. He pressed the button. Jack and Josh closed their eyes. Suddenly, the rocket stopped. Then, it began to descend.

The rocket landed with a soft *thunk* on a purple planet. Then, everything went strangely quiet. "Let's explore," said Jack. So, they put on space suits and stepped out of the rocket doors, as they swished open.

Outside, the purple planet was covered with weird, blue plants. "They look harmless enough," said Josh, stepping forward.

Suddenly, a long, blue tentacle reached out and grabbed his arm.

Jack tried to help Josh. Just then, large, red eyes sprouted from the end of other tentacles. A slimy mouth opened in the middle of the plant. "It's an alien!" cried Josh.

A tentacle grabbed Jack. Gurgling creatures gathered round. They dragged them into a huge cave. Jack and Josh struggled and kicked, but it was no good.

"Where are they taking us?" asked Josh desperately.
"I don't know," replied Jack, "but I don't think it's anywhere good."

The creatures stopped in front of what looked like a huge rock. It was covered in blue slime. Suddenly, two red eyes and a huge mouth opened wide.
"Uh, oh," said Jack. "I think we're about to be dinner!"

Josh suddenly noticed there was a big yellow button on the space suit. "I don't know what this yellow button does, but it's our only hope," said Jack.

They both pressed the buttons. There was a loud roaring sound. They'd activated jet packs fitted to the suits! Suddenly, Jack and Josh whirled into the air. They twisted and turned, then shot out of the cave at full speed. "Hurry!" cried Jack. "They're right behind us!"

Jack and Josh whooshed through the open doors of the rocket and shut
them quickly. Behind them, the angry creatures stretched out their tentacles.
"Quick!" said Josh. "Push the green button!" Jack slammed the button as fast
as he could. There was a rumble and a roar and the rocket blasted off in a
shower of sparks.
"Phew, that was close!" said Jack.

The rocket hurtled through space, all the way back to Earth.
Josh pressed the red button and they landed safely back in the Space Lab.
Amazingly, no one had even noticed they had gone.

Outside, Dad was looking for them. "There you are," he said. "I hope you've
had an exciting time?"
"Oh, yes," said Josh, smiling at Jack. "It's been out of this world!"

The Winning Team

The whistle blew to start the finals of the Soccer League. Smalltown United were playing Ripton Rovers, but Smalltown were nervous. They'd never beaten Ripton before. In fact, Ripton usually made them look useless.

"Come on!" cried Smalltown's star player, Ryan. "We've got to try. Let's give it a whirl!" He dashed forward as a Ripton player kicked the ball, then with one big leap he jumped up to head it.

Ryan swung the ball between the Ripton defenders. He dribbled it all the way down the field. It looked like he was going to score!

Ryan hadn't noticed the biggest, meanest, Ripton player behind him. He knocked Ryan into the air, so that he landed with a bump.

"Ouch!" he cried. "My head!" Ryan was carried off the field on a stretcher. The Smalltown players looked at each other. Without Ryan, they had no chance!

Ripton Rovers were moving really fast. The Smalltown strikers dashed between the Rovers' players, but they couldn't get the ball. Ripton passed to their star player, who kicked the ball towards the goal.

Freddy, the Smalltown goalkeeper dived for the ball, but it was already in the back of the net. The crowd roared and Smalltown felt very silly indeed.

Things got worse and worse for Smalltown. Joey, who was the smallest and fastest team player, dashed in to kick the ball, but got ploughed into the mud by the bigger Ripton players. Ripton raced around Smalltown's defenders and they couldn't do a thing about it.

The whistle finally blew for half time. Smalltown were already 1-0 down. "It's only going to get worse in the second half," the Smalltown players said to each other. "We've got no chance."

As the Smalltown players slouched back to the dressing room, they felt very sad. Ryan was waiting for them. "Don't give up!" he said. "There's still everything to play for."

"We can't do it without you," said Joey. "You're our star player."
"You're all stars," said Ryan. "Just think positively and work together."

"He's right," said Bobby, getting up off the floor. "Come on, let's go out there and give it all we've got!"

The other Smalltown players jumped up. They weren't giving up without a fight.

The whistle blew to start the second half. This time, one of the Smalltown strikers went straight for the ball and won it. Bobby saw the Ripton players racing towards him. He passed the ball before they could reach him. If they worked together, maybe Smalltown did have a hope of winning after all.

"Come on, Smalltown!" cried Ryan from the stands. The crowd began to join in.

The Smalltown players ran down the field as fast as they could. They had the ball and they weren't about to let it go. Behind them, the Ripton players were hot on their heels. They thundered forwards to get the ball. "They're closing in!" cried Joey.

"Come on," said Bobby. "Remember what Ryan said. We just need to think positively and work together!" Suddenly, the Smalltown players began to work like a real team. Franky kicked the ball to Bobby who headed it to Joey, who kicked it to Georgie. Then, with one big kick, Georgie booted the ball into the back of the net.

"GOAL!" The crowd roared and chanted, "SMALLTOWN, SMALLTOWN." It was 1-1 and there were only minutes left.

The Ripton players took control of the ball, but this time the Smalltown players were ready for them. They passed to one another and finally, Joey raced forward. Even though the Ripton players tried to stop him, he saw a tiny gap between them. Joey was so fast, the Ripton keeper never even saw him coming. "GOALLL!"

The final whistle blew and the crowd roared. Smalltown had won! At last they were the winning team.